Praise for
KRISTINE KATHRYN RUSCH'S
DIVING UNIVERSE

"The Diving Universe, conceived by Hugo-Award winning author Kristine [Kathryn] Rusch is a refreshingly new and fleshed out realm of sci-fi action and adventure."
—*Astroguyz*

"Kristine Kathryn Rusch is best known for her Retrieval Artist series, so maybe you've missed her Diving Universe series. If so, it's high time to remedy that oversight."
—*Analog*

"This is classic sci-fi, a well-told tale of dangerous exploration. The first-person narration makes the reader an eye witness to the vast, silent realms of deep space, where even the smallest error will bring disaster. Compellingly human and technically absorbing, the suspense builds to fevered intensity, culminating in an explosive yet plausible conclusion."
—*RT Book Reviews* (Top Pick) on *Diving into the Wreck*

"*[Becalmed]* is quite fascinating and another fine tale from Rusch."
—*SFRevu* on *Becalmed*

The Diving Universe
(Reading Order)

BECALMED

A DIVING UNIVERSE NOVELLA

KRISTINE KATHRYN RUSCH

*wmg*PUBLISHING

Becalmed

Published 2019 by WMG Publishing
www.wmgpublishing.com
First published in *Asimov's SF Magazine,* April/May 2011
Book and cover design copyright © 2019 by WMG Publishing
Cover design by Allyson Longueira/WMG Publishing
Cover art copyright © Glazyuk/Dreamstime
ISBN-13: 978-1-56146-298-8
ISBN-10: 1-56146-298-5

BECALMED

A DIVING UNIVERSE NOVELLA

Here's what they tell you when you want to leave the Fleet:

Stay behind. Don't get back on the ship, not even to retrieve your things. Have someone bring the important items to you.

Check to see if any of your friends or any members of your family want to leave as well. Don't force them. For most of us, the ship is and has always been home. Life on a planet—any planet—is different. Very different. So different that some can't handle it, even if they think they can.

Don't go to a base. Don't ask to be dropped off. Stay. Create a new life with the grateful people you've saved/helped/rescued.

Become someone else.

They tell us these things before each mission and then again as one is ending. They tell us these things so that we can make the right choice for us, the right choice for the ship. The right choice for everyone.

They do this because they used to forbid us from leaving. We were of the ship, they'd say. We were part of the Fleet. We were specially chosen, specially bred.

We were, they said, able to overcome anything.

But that wasn't true. Even with ships built for five hundred people, there is no room for one slowly devolving intellect, one emotionally unstable but highly trained individual.

No room for the crazy, the sick, or the absolutely terrified.

The key, however, is finding that person. Figuring out who she is.

And what to do about her.

2

IT HAD BEEN A SLAUGHTER. TWENTY-SEVEN OF US, AND only three survived.

I am one of the survivors.

And that is all I know.

I sit on the window seat in my living area, staring out the portal. I had asked, back when I got promoted the very first time, to have an apartment on the outer edges of the ship. I'd been told apartments that brushed against the exterior were dangerous, that if the ship sustained serious damage I could lose everything.

But I like looking out the portal—a real portal, not a wall screen, not some kind of entertainment—at space as it is at this moment.

But I do not look into space.

Instead, I have activated a small section of my wall screen. I read and reread the regulations. I translate them into different languages. I have the ship's computer recite them to me. I have the children's school programs explain them.

The upshot is the same:

I should leave. I should never have come back to the ship. That was my mistake.

Theirs was to keep me and not ask me to remain planetside.

These errors make me nervous. They make me wonder what will happen next, and that is unusual. The ship thrives on structure. Structure comes from following a schedule, following the rules, following long-established traditions.

Tradition dictates an announcement to the entire crew at the beginning and end of each mission: the always familiar, easily quotable regulations about disembarking at the next stop, about leaving if you can no longer perform your duties.

We should have gotten that announcement as soon as the *anacapa* drive delivered us to this fold in space. We have been here too long.

Even I know that.

Each ship in the Fleet has an *anacapa* drive. The drive works also works as a cloak, although my former husband objects to that term. If the *Ivoire* is under attack, the captain activates the *anacapa* drive, which moves us into foldspace. We stay in foldspace only a moment, then return to our original position seconds or hours later, depending on the manner in which the navigators programmed the *anacapa*. Sometimes, in a battle, seconds are all you need. The enemy ship moves; we do not. We vanish for a moment. Then we reappear, behind them.

Or we don't reappear for hours, and they think us long gone.

Either way, we are only in foldspace for a moment.

We have been in this foldspace for days.

I bring my feet onto the window seat, press my thighs against my breasts, and rest my head on my knees.

No one will tell me anything. I am shaky and emotional, unable to remember. Unable to think clearly about anything.

And for a woman who has spent her entire life thinking, this change terrifies me most of all.

3

AFTER FOUR SHIP DAYS, THEY OPEN MY APARTMENT DOOR.

They don't knock. They override the locks—locks I've programmed in my paranoia.

I don't recognize them, although I recognize their gold uniforms.

Medical Evaluation Unit: Psychological and Emotional Stress Department.

How many people have I sent to them over the years? How smug have I felt when the medics in the gold uniforms take troublesome workers from my linguistic unit?

Now they've come for me—four Ship Days after we entered this foldspace, ten Ship Days after I was medivacked from our makeshift headquarters on Ukhanda, nine Ship Days after they asked what the Quurzod had done and I answered, "To my knowledge, nothing at all."

To my knowledge.

Which is terrifyingly incomplete.

Two men and a woman stand in my doorway. I don't recognize any of them. Clearly, they were never on the teams that took workers from my section.

The woman is the spokesman. She introduces herself. The name washes over me even though I try to catch it, hang onto it, remember it.

Her spiel isn't what I expect. I expected the standard: *You have the right to refuse treatment. You have the right to remain in your apartment until we reach planetside. You have the right to your own medical professional.*

Instead, she says, "You are about to undergo a battery of psychological tests. Some will prove exceedingly difficult and/or uncomfortable. Some are designed to retrieve memories you—or something around you—have blocked. These tests will provide us with the truth as you understand it. They will also show if you still retain what is commonly known of as your sanity. Do you understand?"

Oh, I understand. I should be relieved by this, but I am not. I swallow uncontrollably. I am shaking.

What I want to say, what I'm trying not to say, is that I don't want to remember. I don't want to know.

Just charge me and be done with it.

Take me back to Ukhanda and leave me there, like you were supposed to.

Forget I even exist.

"Do you understand?" she asks again.

One of the men stares at me, as if he's trying to figure out whether or not I can speak. I can speak in fifteen languages, and twenty-three different dialects. I can understand sixty languages, albeit some imperfectly.

I can speak. And I do understand. I just don't want to admit it.

She starts, "Do you—"

"Yes," I say, thinking that will end her spiel.

But it doesn't.

"You will want an advocate," she says. "That can be a friend, a family member, or a professional. We can provide you with a list of professional advocates or you can contact one on your own."

I dry swallow again. An advocate? I'd heard this in legal matters, but not in psychological ones.

What did I do on Ukhanda?

Do I know?

Do they?

"Am I in serious trouble?" I ask.

For a moment, the woman's eyes soften. I sense compassion. But then, I might be searching for it.

Or seeing it where it does not exist.

"Yes," she says.

"Could it damage my family?" I ask.

"Yes," she says.

I have left my family out of this so far. I haven't contacted them since my return. Nor have I allowed any of them to contact me, although they've tried. I have shut them out, changed the contact codes, refused to acknowledge them when they've been outside my door.

Now I feel a bit of comfort—what I had seen as selfish behavior will benefit them after all.

"I'm not going with you until I have an advocate," I say.

"Good choice," she says, and waits while I contact the best advocate we have.

4

I HAVE NEVER MET MY ADVOCATE BEFORE, BUT I HAVE followed her work for nearly a decade. Legal matters onboard ship are often petty, but they provide real-time entertainment of a kind that most fictions can't.

And when the legal matters spill into the Fleet, then the entertainment ratchets up.

Leona Shearing has handled some of the biggest intraFleet controversies, but she keeps her hand in on the smaller cases, mostly, she tells me when she arrives at my apartment, because she likes to remain busy. IntraFleet controversies happen only rarely. Smaller, shipboard cases occur every day.

She acts as if I'm a smaller shipboard case. I don't disabuse her of this notion, although she is surprised that three medical personnel have come to take me away, not the usual two.

She is a flamboyant woman who wears her hair down. She prefers flowing garments, unusual clothing in the Fleet, where most every department has its own uniform and the uniforms differ only by color. She does not work for the Fleet. She runs her own business. All the advocates have their own businesses, as do some of the tutors scattered across the ships. Specialists on the *Sante* often work privately as well, and so do many of the restaurateurs on the *Brazza*.

Still, working for someone other than the Fleet is unusual, and risky. Many do not acknowledge their difference, wearing clothing that suggests a uniform. Leona Shearing accentuates her difference with her clothing and her hair. Her manner, however, is strictly professional.

She interviews me briefly—asking my name, my rank, my position, as if she's checking to see if I am of sound mind. Then she turns to the three medical personnel, who have not left the room, and asks them why they didn't just send for me.

"She needs to be escorted," the woman says.

"You only need two people for that," Leona says.

"One stays. We have occasion to search the apartment."

She frowns, then narrows her eyes as she looks at me. "Did you let them in here?"

"No," I say. "They overrode the codes."

She stands. "You need to tell me what she's being accused of."

"She ran a team of twenty-seven to study the Quurzod," the woman says. "Only three returned."

"I assume she's one of the three who returned," Leona says.

"Yes," the woman says.

"The twenty-four are dead?" Leona asks.

"We believe so," the woman says.

"You don't know?" Leona asks.

"We have not verified the deaths," the woman says.

Something whispers across my brain, too fast for me to catch it.

"Are the other two survivors being investigated?" Leona says.

"No," the woman says.

"Why not?" Leona asks.

The woman looks at me. "She's the only one who broke away from the group."

My stomach clenches. I have to will my hands not to form fists. I lean against the portal, unable to look at the strangeness of space.

"So?" Leona says.

"So she's the only one we found covered in blood," the woman says.

I bite my lower lip. Technically, they didn't find me. Technically, I staggered into a nearby village, and the villagers contacted the ship.

Technically, I found them.

"I still don't see the issue," Leona asks. "I'm sure you tested the blood. From your tone and her appearance, I'm gathering that it wasn't all hers."

"None of it was hers," the woman says.

I glance at Leona. I expect her to look at me, then get up and nod toward me regretfully, to tell me that I no longer deserve her services. But she doesn't look in my direction at all.

Instead, she says to the woman, "Correct me if I'm wrong, but aren't we at war with the Quurzod?"

"We weren't then," the woman says.

"We weren't friendly," Leona says. "We were there at the request of the Xenth, to investigate claims of genocide, were we not?"

The woman stiffens. So do I. I don't remember genocide. I don't remember going planetside.

I don't remember anything except the heat, the dry air. The stench of drying blood.

"We weren't at war yet," the woman says primly.

"We were in unfriendly territory, trying to change the balance of power," Leona says. "That's as close as you can get without declaring hostilities."

The woman's mouth thins. The men haven't moved. It's as if the conversation is going on in another room.

I try not to look at them. I try not to look at any of them.

"I am not a politician," the woman says. "I'm not sure at what stage a war becomes a war."

"Perhaps at the first sign of bloodshed," Leona says.

"I think that's too simplistic," the woman says.

"I thought you weren't a politician," Leona says.

They stare at each other. My heart pounds. I'm not sure what my advocate is playing at.

The woman takes a deep breath. "They say she caused the deaths."

"Who says?" Leona asks, and I hear a new note in her voice. Triumph? Had she been fishing for information? Was that why she goaded the medics?

"The other two," the woman says.

"The other two," Leona says. "Who weren't covered in blood."

"Yes," the woman says.

"Who didn't stagger out of the desert alone, dehydrated, and nearly dead," Leona says.

Was I nearly dead? I don't remember that. I just remember how the heat served up mirages like water, how the air had so much dust it seemed like a live thing, how my skin burned to the touch.

"What were they doing while their colleagues were dying?" Leona says.

The woman gets that prim look again. "I don't know," she says. "You'll have to ask them."

She's lying. She knows.

My stomach is a hard knot. I rest one hand against it, hoping to soothe it.

"If you suspect her of a heinous crime," Leona says, "why did you let her back on ship?"

"She has the captain's protection," the woman says.

I wince. I didn't ask for that. He shouldn't be involved.

"The captain can't protect her," Leona says. "He should know that. If she's done something wrong, she gets punished—planetside."

"We're at war," the woman says. "We couldn't keep our people planetside."

"Then we leave her and bring the innocents back," Leona says.

I close my eyes. She's right. That's what the regulations say. I shouldn't be here.

"The captain can't change the regulations," Leona says. She's clearly pushing something, but what I don't know.

"Actually," the woman says, "that's a gray area. We have two policies, the modern and the ancient. Both apply in this case."

Leona frowns. She doesn't agree. Isn't it her business to know the regulations? Isn't she the expert in them, like I'm the expert in languages?

"No one gets left behind," the woman says. "That's the ancient regulation. No matter how criminal, how perverted, how sick, no one gets left behind."

She looks at me as she says those things and she has that look in her eyes again. What I had initially taken for sympathy is something else. Fear? Disgust?

"The captain chose to follow that regulation," the woman says.

"Is that why he didn't run the announcement?" I ask.

"I don't presume to know why the captain does what he does," the woman says. "He should have left you behind."

"I know," I say.

Leona frowns at me and even though I don't know her, I can read her expression. *Shut up. Let me talk. I'm your advocate. Let me advocate.*

"You want to tell me why he didn't?" the woman asks.

I shrug one shoulder. I don't honestly know. I haven't talked to him. Since I got back, the entire Fleet's been attacked. We've moved, been hit, then moved to foldspace. I suspect the captain's been busy.

"Are you sure it was him who ordered me back?" I ask.

"Enough," Leona says. "We can talk all night, but until we have facts, I can't help you. And I need to know what you want. I know what they want. They want to test you."

She's looking at me, and her eyes hold no emotion at all. Only a few people can effectively do that. She's clearly learned it over the course of her career. She doesn't know what to think of me, and she doesn't want me to know that.

She wants me to think she's on my side.

As if I know what my side is.

"I can block the tests," she says.

My heart leaps as she says this, but I dry swallow yet again. I am afraid of the tests. I am afraid of what they will reveal. I am afraid of what they won't reveal.

"Why don't you study my case," I say, sounding calm and logical, which I am not, "and then we'll decide what to do."

"We need to take her out of the residential wing," the woman says. "She's dangerous."

"We don't know that," Leona says.

"We can assume," the woman says.

Leona turns back to her. Leona's expression changes, from that flat look she gives me to something akin to anger. Only I'm not sure that emotion is real either.

"From my understanding," Leona says, "she's been here for days. If she was going to snap, she would have already. Lock the doors, post a guard, put some kind of monitor on her. But leave her here. You know as well as I do that familiarity provides comfort."

But the apartment isn't familiar.

Well, part of it is. The furniture, the mementos that I have brought from previous trips, my bedding, my clothing.

But the view from the portal—it's unfamiliar, and bound to become more so.

If I don't have to look outside the ship, I might feel better.

"Do you have portals in the evaluation ward?" I ask the woman.

"Yes," she says.

So outside lurks here, there, in any place they'd take me.

I let out a shaky sigh. "Then I'll stay here."

As if the decision is sane.

As if I am.

As if I would know the difference.

5

THEY ALL LEAVE ME, LEONA WHO IS OFF TO DO RESEARCH, the three medical personnel. They've posted guards, just like Leona told them to, and they made a point of letting me know. The guards—both big, muscular men—displayed the laser pistols attached to their hips and gave me a stern look.

The warning was clear. If I tried to leave, they'd shoot.

If I tried to leave.

Which I'm not going to do.

Maybe they're the ones who aren't thinking. I'm the one who locked myself in my apartment. I'm the one who has hidden from everyone I love.

My twin sister Deirdre has left me increasingly urgent messages, using her technical skills to override the protections I've put on my private communications. She is worried, she says. She has heard horrible things, she says. She wants to see me, she says.

Too bad. I don't want to see her.

I don't want to see anyone.

Not even Coop.

Jonathon Cooper, our captain. My former husband. He looks like a captain of the Fleet should. He's tall, broad-shouldered, dark haired, handsome, and oh, so intelligent.

We married young and I was going to have a thousand babies, or maybe the acceptable two. But the babies never happened. Every time I got pregnant, I had to go planetside on some mission or another, and every time, I lost them.

The prenatal unit offered to harbor the fetuses for me, so that my risky job wouldn't have an impact on my children, but Coop didn't like the idea. For a man who has attached himself to a machine—loving the *Ivoire* more than anyone, anything else—he has very old-fashioned views about children. He believes that a child housed in a fetal unit will not have the warmth and compassion, the ability to bond with others, that regular humans do.

He might be right; Lord knows, he's shown me a lot of studies, all from the Fleet, all from various points in our history, all very scientific.

I know this, but I also know that gestating a child in the woman is no guarantee either. The fetus gets exposed to whatever the woman gets exposed to, and sometimes that exposure is toxic or strange or just plain terrifying.

Dry, dry sand. Heat so extreme that my skin aches. The blood has dried on my skin and it stinks, rotting, even as it's attached to me. But I cannot get it off. I don't have the water to drink, let alone any to clean myself. I don't have—

I stand up. My face feels flushed, my skin tight with dried blood.

I don't want to remember.

I put my hands on my cheeks. I was thinking about Coop. Coop and the babies that never were, and our perennial argument, and the way that he looks at me, even now, as if I have broken his heart.

We still love each other. But we are no longer *in love* with each other. If we ever were in love with each other.

I think we were in love with the idea of each other. Coop is a bona fide hero, a man who rushes in when he should hang back, who has saved countless lives, who always puts others first and rarely thinks of himself.

I'm the intellectual, the collected one, the one who thinks before she acts—who thinks in many languages before she acts. Coop has always been intrigued by my skills, my ability to make myself understood, to put myself in the place of another culture, another person, to become someone I'm not, even if only for a few minutes.

There is too much Coop to subsume into another human being, even for a moment. I'm beginning to understand that there is not enough me, and perhaps that's why I can completely vanish into another perspective, because mine is so fragile, so very frail.

Or is it? Coop always says I have a firm core. He may be right. That may be why I am still here—alive, one of three survivors. But that might also be why I can't remember, why I feel my brains leaking out of my skull, why my memory skips as if it were a rock skimming a clear mountain lake.

I am standing in the middle of my apartment, back to the portal, in foldspace, guards outside my door, my memory gone. I am here because my former husband still loves me too much to sacrifice me for the good of the ship, even though he makes up other reasons. Ancient regulations versus new regulations. Silly, that. He just can't abide sending me to the middle of that planet, as the war has heated up, a war we started.

Twenty-four died.

I survived.

Along with two others.

Whom I can't remember.

Just like I can't remember what happened to everybody else.

6

"SOMETHING ODD IS HAPPENING HERE," I SAY TO LEONA. I'm looking out my portal at foldspace. At least I think it's foldspace.

I recognize nothing out there, and neither does my computer. When I catch a moment, a moment when I can concentrate, I use my apartment computer, trying to figure out where we are. I have to use the information stored on the computer itself; the ship has cut me off. I can't get into any systems, even informational ones.

The message system doesn't even work properly. If I want to send a message to anyone other than the medical evaluation unit or Leona, I have to send it through the approval system. Someone else will listen to my complaints, read my notes, see my anxious face.

Rather than let that happen, I don't send messages.

Not that I feel like communicating anyway.

"Yes, something odd is happening," Leona says. "You're essentially imprisoned in your own apartment."

She sounds offended by this, which strikes me as strange. I'm not offended. I turn.

She's sitting at my table, her own portable notebook on her lap. Her dark hair is up, and she's wearing a formal tunic with matching pants.

"I'm not talking about me," I say, sweeping a hand toward the portal. "Something odd is happening on the ship. To the ship. I don't know where we are."

Her expression freezes as if I've said something wrong.

"Is this something you're not supposed to tell me?" I ask.

She shakes her head. "I forgot, that's all. You can't access the news."

Shipboard news is an outside system. I've never really paid attention anyway, except when I need to for my work, and even then, I'm not really watching. I'm listening—not to what's going on, but to how it's expressed.

I am the ship's senior linguist, a position as important as the captain's in its own way. Strange that I haven't thought of that since I've come back. I haven't identified myself as a linguist at all. I haven't missed the interplay of languages, the way that the same sentence in one language can mean something completely different when translated word-for-word into another.

Context, subtext, word origins, emotions, all contained in one little phrase, one little word. The difference between "an" and "the" can alter meaning dramatically.

And it's my job to know these subtleties in every language I specialize in. It's my job to understand them in the new languages I encounter. It's my job to make sure we can all communicate clearly, because the basis of diplomacy isn't action, it's words.

Words, words, words.

"You've gone pale," Leona says. "Do you need to sit down?"

"No." I walk back to the portal. It's space-black out there—not quite total darkness. The universe has its own light, and it's lovely, most of the time. But usually you can see the source—the star in the distance, the reflection off clouds protecting a planet's atmosphere.

I see nothing.

I have seen nothing for days.

I sometimes check my own eyesight to see if the problem is inside my head.

(I'm so afraid it is inside my head.)

"What's the news?" I ask, even though I'm no longer sure I want to know.

She pauses. I turn. She's frowning. It's an expression I didn't expect to see on her face. She's not someone who lets her emotions near the surface.

I have a clear sense of how terrified she is, and how unwilling she is to admit it.

Although I can't tell you why I feel that way. I can't tell you how I know.

I just do.

Something subtle then, something subtle like the things I specialize in.

"The *anacapa* malfunctioned," she says. "We're becalmed."

Becalmed. A nautical term, adapted from Earth, in the days before ships sailed the heavens. In those days, ships sailed the waters, the seas, they were called, and being becalmed was dangerous.

Sailing ships had no engines. They were powered by the wind. And when the wind was gone, the ship didn't move. Sometimes, way out at sea, a becalmed ship wouldn't move for days, weeks, and the men—it was always men—on board would die.

Some say they died from thirst or lack of food.

But other accounts say that men who were becalmed died because conditions had driven them insane.

"Becalmed," I repeat, and sink into a nearby chair. My heart rate has increased.

Leona watches me, as if she's afraid of what the news will do to me.

She should be.

The Fleet adopted the word "becalmed" because it's the best way to describe being stuck in foldspace. The *anacapa* malfunctions, and we can't get back. It has happened throughout our history.

Ships get lost, some because they're becalmed. What no one knows, what no one can figure out, is if they're stuck in an alternate universe or in the actual fold of space itself.

If there is an actual fold of space.

We don't know—at least those of us who are in no real need to know. Coop probably knows. He's probably doing everything he can.

"Has he sent a distress?" I ask, because I can't not ask. I have to know, even though I do know. Of course, Coop sent a distress. Of course, he's run through procedure. Of course, he's done everything he can do.

"Several," she says.

"And?"

"No one is responding." She looks at her well-manicured hand. "Some believe that our comm system is down."

I'm an expert in the comm system. I have to be. Because if the comm techs are incapacitated, someone from the linguistic staff still has to communicate to others. So my technical training—my *mechanical* training, to use another old Earth term—is in comm systems. I'm as good (maybe better) than Coop's chief communications officer.

And no one has called me.

Maybe that's why I haven't heard any announcement. Not because Coop couldn't leave me behind, but because another emergency superseded mine.

Maybe I'm forgotten, a byproduct, something the junior members of the staff must deal with until the regular members have time to think about me.

"I have comm system expertise," I say, again, because I can't not say it.

"I know," Leona says.

But she says no more.

"When did the *anacapa* malfunction?" I ask.

She looks at me, as if I should remember. I don't remember.

"We were outgunned," she says. "The Quurzod were right behind us. They fired as we engaged the *anacapa*.

We suffered a lot of damage, and that's when they think the drive malfunctioned."

This does not reassure me, which irritates me. Apparently I'd been hoping for reassurance.

"We don't know?" I ask.

She shakes her head. "It's hard to do assessments out here. They want to go to a base, but no base is answering. We have limited equipment, limited supplies. We're on rations—."

She stops herself.

I stand up again. I'm like a child's toy—up, down, up, down. I can't stay still for a moment.

"We don't need to be on rations," I say. "We have enough supplies to last years."

Then it's my turn to freeze. We have enough supplies to last years if we know where we are. If we know where we're going. If we know we can get resupplied.

"They think no one will find us, don't they?" I whisper. "They think we're on our own."

She nods. Just once, as if nodding more than once would be too much acknowledgement, would make us complicit in something.

"They don't know where we are, do they?" I ask.

She shrugs, but it isn't a casual gesture. It's a frustrated gesture.

Shrugs are part of communication. The nuances of shrugs are something I have learned over time.

"They need me," I say.

"Yes," she says. "They do."

But she doesn't move, and she doesn't say any more. She's eloquent in her silences.

They need me, but they haven't come for me. They believe I can't help them, because I'm somehow damaged, because I've done something wrong.

"Is that why the medical evaluation team came?" I say. "To get me back to work?"

She looks at that manicured hand again. She doesn't reply. Is that a no? Suddenly, for all my training in subtlety, all I've learned about reading gestures, I can't tell.

Finally, she takes a breath. She was steeling herself to talk with me. She isn't sure I should hear this, but she's going to tell me anyway.

"Do you know why the Quurzod came after us so vehemently?" she asks.

"No." I don't remember much after staggering into that village, after someone gasped, pulled me aside, touched my caked skin.

I collapsed, and woke up on a bed, hooked up to an IV, liquid applied directly into the veins because I couldn't drink on my own. I woke up later in the hospital wing on the *Ivoire*, refreshed, no longer burned, my skin smooth and clean and my mouth no longer dry.

I have no idea how I got there, only that I did.

"The Quurzod came because of you," she says.

I look at her.

"We lost twenty-four," she says. "They lost more."

I cannot move. "How many more?"

She shrugs—oh, so eloquent. Not frustrated this time, but an I-don't-know shrug, an is-an-exact-number-really-important? shrug. "You tell me."

I have to force myself to breathe. "You're saying it's my fault?"

"I'm not saying anything," she says.

But she is. Oh, she is.

Because I am responsible for communications, language, *diplomacy*.

If we went in twenty-seven strong—and we did—that means we went in as a team. A planetside team usually has thirty, but I remember—(do I? Or am I making this up?)—that we lost three because they couldn't stomach the Quurzod.

Not that the Quurzod are so different from us. We haven't discovered any aliens in our travels—not true aliens, anyway, not aliens in the way that we define them, as sentient creatures who build and create and form attachments like we do. We've found strange creatures and even stranger plants, but nothing like the human race.

Although we have found humans throughout our centuries of travel. Thousands and thousands of humans. Each with different languages, different skills, different levels of development.

But exactly the same—emotional, callous, brilliant, sad—capable of great good and great violence, often within the same culture.

The Quurzod—the Quurzod, oh, I remember the briefings, snatches of the briefings at any rate. They make an art out of violence. They kill and maim and do so with great relish. When they committed genocide against the Xenth, they did so with psychopathic glee—killing children in front of parents, torturing loved ones, experimenting to see what kind of punishment a human body could take before it had enough and simply quit.

The stories distressed my team. Three couldn't face the Quurzod.

It makes no sense. If I started this, then that was all the more reason to leave me behind. We're taught from childhood that sacrifices are necessary.

We travel in a fleet of ships 500 strong. We split off for various missions, and sometimes we sacrifice an entire ship if we have to. An individual life—one of at least 500 lives on the *Ivoire* alone—means less than the mission.

The mission: to provide assistance throughout the known universe. We are the good guys, the rescuers; we are the ones who make the wrongs right. We do what we can, interfere if we must, help when we're needed.

And when we make mistakes, we make them right.

We don't run.

It seems like we ran.

"I want to talk to Coop," I say.

Leona shakes her head. "Not until you can tell us what happened."

"Then I should let the medical evaluation unit run their tests."

Her head shaking becomes more pronounced. "You can't. We need truth here, not legal tricks."

"Tricks?" I say. "They'll be using equipment, running diagnostics—"

"Asking you questions, putting memories in your head." She runs her hand over her notebook. "We'll wait until your own memories return."

She looks at the portal, then back at me.

"After all," she says dismally. "We have time."

7

SOMETIMES I SLEEP. THE BODY DEMANDS IT, AND WHEN it can no longer function without sleep, I doze wherever I am.

I have fallen asleep on the divan. I love the divan. I have put it in the center of my living area, where most people have group seating. But I never hold meetings here.

I used to study on it, let words dance around me as I spoke them. They'd turn red if I pronounced something wrong, and they'd vanish if spoken correctly. I loved word dancing. I loved study.

Now I lie on the divan and I stare out the portal at all that nothing, not thinking at all. Words don't even run through my head. I know I've been thinking, but I cannot articulate what the thoughts are.

Yet as I fall asleep, I know I am asleep. I feel the divan beneath me, note that the apartment is a bit too cold, think I should tell the apartment's system to adjust the heat. Or I should grab a blanket from the bedroom. I should be comfortable.

But I am not. I claw my way through a pile of stinky, sticky flesh. Arms move, legs flop, a head turns toward me, eyes gone. I force myself not to look. I am climbing people and I know that if I don't I will die.

I jerk awake, shudder, trying to get the images from my head. Leona wants me to remember.

I don't.

I get up and take a blanket off my bed. Then I stop and look at the wall, the only wall I have decorated.

An old blanket—a quilt, to use the proper term—adds color to the room. Pinks and reds and glorious blues, mixed together in a wedding ring pattern. The quilt has been in my family for generations, given, my mother said, to an ancestor as the Fleet embarked from Earth itself.

I don't know for certain because I've never tested the quilt. I keep it out of harsh light. It's preservation framed, done by my grandmother, and its beauty should remind us of tradition, of homes we'll never see again, of family.

I have cousins on other ships in the Fleet, family, some distant in corridors down the way. We are not close. My sister has a daughter, and if I never have children, this quilt will go to her.

I wrap the blanket around myself and walk back to the divan. I recline on it again, look out the portal, see that brightly lit blackness, threatening starshine, but not delivering it.

And—

I'm still climbing. The sunlight beats down on me, the heat nearly unbearable. I've been praying for the wind to stop since I got here, but now that it has, I want it back, if only to get rid of the insects and the stench.

I am the only one alive. I do not want to look but I do—faces, eyes especially, eyes glazed over and an odd white. Blood everywhere. I climb, standing on people, and if I look up, I can see an edge to the pit I am in.

I stop, listen, hear only my ragged breathing. If I can hear it, someone else can hear it too. Someone lurking out there. Someone who will—

I can't do it this way. There is no comfort in this apartment, in these rooms. If this is a memory, then I do not want to be alone with it.

If it is a nightmare, I want it banished.

If it is an example of how I will live from now on, I cannot. I will not. I will die before I continue like this.

I contact Leona. Her face appears on my wall screen, looking concerned. I do not give her time to speak.

I say, "I'm going to have the evaluations."

And then I sever the link.

8

THE GUARDS ESCORT ME TO THE MEDICAL UNIT. I'M NOT used to being escorted. I'm used to leading. But these two men, both bigger than me, walk beside me, brushing against me, making it clear that I'm in their power.

They lead me down one of the main corridors in the ship, so it's wide enough for people to pass us. Everyone who does averts their eyes, partly because I no longer look like me, and partly because I'm being escorted.

Just because there are five hundred of us on the ship doesn't mean we all know each other. Some of us apprenticed on other ships. Some of us grew up elsewhere in the Fleet. I met Coop on the *Brazza*, when we were going to school. That we both ended up on the senior staff of the *Ivoire* had less to do with our designs than with our abilities, and a gap in leadership at the *Ivoire* at the time.

Back then I was young enough not to realize that I profited from other people's failures. I notice now.

Just like I'm being noticed, even though people are looking away. They see a crazed woman, hair down, so distracted she forgot to put on shoes before she told the guards she wanted to go to the medical unit. I'm walking through the cold corridors with bare feet, wearing a knee-length white shirt and matching pants—my comfort clothes—in a place where almost everyone else is in uniform.

The medical evaluation unit is on the fifth level of the medical wing. Everything here is as white as my clothing, with nanobits that keep the walls and floors clean. My bare feet leave footprints that get erased by the nanobits after just a moment. The dirt from the guards' shoes evaporates as quickly as well.

The staff working in the medical unit must work one week in other parts of the ship. This area is too sterile for good human health, and the medical personnel who do not leave find themselves developing allergies and sensitivities to the most normal things—like skin cells and cooking oils.

I've put in time in the medical unit as well—all of the linguists do as part of our training. We program the medical database with medical terms from any new language we've learned. We also train the staff to speak the most rudimentary forms of many languages—enough to ask after another person's health—and to understand the answers.

The guards lead me to the fifth level. There a woman waits for me. She's not the woman who invaded my apartment. Nor is she anyone I know.

She's tiny, with raven-black hair, black eyes, and a straight line for a mouth. She extends her hand.

"I'm Jill Bannerman," she says. "I'll help you through the evaluation."

"I can't do anything until my advocate gets here," I say. The words come out awkward and ungracious. I'm excellent at being accommodating, at saying the right thing at the right time—or I used to be.

"I know," Bannerman says. "I'll get you ready, and then we'll wait for her. She should be here shortly."

I don't know what ready means. It makes me nervous. I shake my head. "I'd like to wait."

"All right," she says, as if she expected that. "Sit here. We'll get started as soon as she arrives."

She leads me to an orange chair that curves around my body as I sit. I'm so paranoid that I wonder if it's taking readings from me.

But the *Ivoire*—the Fleet, actually—has privacy laws. Even if this chair records information off me, no one can use the information without my permission.

Have I given permission by agreeing to the evaluation? I have no idea. I should have checked with Leona first.

That's what she'll say.

Jill Bannerman speaks softly to my guards, then she leaves the room. The guards move out of the main area and back outside the doors. I'm alone in a room with half a dozen chairs, with walls that reset themselves, and furniture that changes color every ten minutes. First orange, then red, then mauve, then purple, then blue. I watch the furniture, a bit unnerved by it all.

There is nothing else to watch, no entertainment, no open portals, no other people. Just me and the constantly changing furniture.

I tuck my cold feet underneath my legs and make myself breathe deeply. I want to tap my fingertips on the chair, but someone will read that as nervousness, I'm sure. I don't know why I'm worried that they will notice—it's hard to miss, and if the system is recording my vital signs, the nervousness will show in my elevated heart rate, my slightly higher-than-normal blood pressure, and even in my breathing.

The only thing I'm not doing right now is regretting my decision. I'm suddenly quite happy to be out of my apartment. I hadn't realized how claustrophobic I felt in it, how shut down I had been.

How terrified.

The doors slide open and Leona sweeps in. Her green tunic changes the color scheme in the room. Now the chairs float through forest colors—green, dark green, blue-green, blue. She slides into a chair across from me.

"We can still leave," she says.

I shake my head.

"We need a consult, and we can't have it here," she says.

So I *am* being monitored. "I'm doing this," I say.

"You made that clear," she says. "Now we determine how to do it best for you."

Whatever that means.

"There's a privacy room just over there," she says. "We're using it."

I've read up on advocacy. She's not supposed to give me orders. She's supposed to follow mine. But she's worried and I'm not strong enough to fight her. Besides, I'm not leaving the medical evaluation unit. I'm just stepping into a private room for a few minutes to consult with my advocate.

I don't have to take her advice.

She touches the wall and a door slides open. I hadn't noticed it while I was waiting, distracted (apparently) by the constantly changing furniture.

This room is also white with a black conference table that has grown out of the floor. Two chairs sit side by side. I suppose if more people walk in, more chairs will grow out of their storage spots on the floor.

The overhead lights spotlight the chairs and nearby, coffee brews as if someone set it up for us.

Leona ignores it, but I help myself. As I touch the coffee pot, pastries slide in from the far wall. Pastries and an entire plate of fruit, some of it exotic.

"I thought we're on rations," I say to her.

"We are, but maybe the medical wing is exempt."

The food gets her up and she stacks a plate with strudels and Danishes and things I don't even have a name for. I grab a banana that looks like it came from one of the hydroponics bays, and something with lots of frosting and raisins.

My stomach actually growls. I'm not sure when the last time I ate was.

We sit down with our food and our coffees, suddenly so civilized.

She picks up one of the Danishes, but doesn't take a bite. "I know I can't change your mind, but I want you to know what's at risk."

I eat the banana first. It's green and chewy, not really ripe, almost sour. I don't care. It feels like the first food I've eaten in years, even though it's not.

"I found out why they brought you back to the ship," Leona says.

That, of all things, catches my attention. It sounds ominous.

"Why?"

"They need to know what happened planetside. They need to know if it's our fault."

A shiver runs down my back. If it's our fault. Of course it's our fault. The Fleet meddles. That's what we do.

"What do the other two survivors say?" I ask.

She doesn't look at me. Instead she takes a bite of that Danish and eats slowly. I want to push her on this. I want her to tell me everything right now.

But some vestiges of my training remain. I sit and watch, counting silently to myself because it's the only way I can keep still.

Stillness used to be my best weapon. I could wait for anyone. I could listen forever, and learn, without making a move.

But I seem to have lost that ability. I'm restless now, and time feels like it has sped up. Even though I know it has only taken a moment for her to eat that small bite of pastry, it feels as if she has taken an hour.

"What do they say?" I ask because I can't wait any longer. So much for stillness.

"I don't know," she says. "I haven't spoken to them directly."

"But you know," I press.

She shrugs a shoulder—a sorry-said-all-I-can shrug.

Then she sets the pastry down and wipes her hand on a small napkin. "Look," she says. "If that mess turns out to be our fault, then you'll probably be executed. Now do you see why I don't want you to do this?"

"I need to do this," I say softly.

"Why?" she asks.

"The memories are coming back. I can't experience them on my own. It's better if they all come back at once."

She stares at me, and then sighs. "I'll see what I can do," she says, and leaves.

9

I SIT IN THAT ROOM FOR WHAT FEELS LIKE FOREVER, but really is only about an hour. There is a bathroom next to the service area, and I'm able to use that, but I'm not able to leave the room itself. I pace. I count to ten in fifteen languages. Then in six more. And then I start over because I can't remember all the languages I just tried.

I've just started counting to one hundred when Leona returns.

"Jill Bannerman is outside," Leona says. "When she comes in here, you tell her what you told me about not being able to cope. Be dramatic. The more threatened you feel the better."

"I won't be lying," I say. "I can't do this alone."

Those words are so inadequate. If I close my eyes, I can feel the heat, the blood drying on my skin, the bodies rolling beneath my hands. I can't sit still with that. I have to move. And the more of it that comes back to me, the more movement I need to make.

"You tell her that," Leona says. "Make it very clear that this is a medical issue."

"Why?" I ask.

"Because that gives you legal protection. You'll be considered a patient, not a criminal. If they had taken you that afternoon when you called me, you'd've been a criminal. Just like you would have been if you hadn't waited for me today. This way, you'll be able to say anything, do anything, and it won't come out in a legal proceeding. At least not in detail. The ship's staff can have an advocate in the room, and he can testify to what you say, but it won't have the force of your testimony. It can only be used to start an investigation, which they're already running."

I stare at her. She thinks I've done something wrong. They all seem to think I've done something wrong.

Is that why I can't remember?

"Before you decide," she says, "this is your last chance to go back to your apartment. You can do this on your own and no one will ever have to know."

My stomach clenches. "And then what?"

"What do you mean?"

"Will I ever be able to leave my apartment? Will I be able to return to my duties?"

She shakes her head. "You'll be alive. Isn't that enough?"

I think about the view from my portal. Stuck in fold-space with nothing to see. The same walls, a different view, if we're lucky, but the same walls for the rest of my life. No more languages. No more work.

No more friends or family.

Just me. Alive. In my apartment.

Becalmed.

"Send her in," I say, "and I'll tell her the truth."

***

THE TRUTH IS THAT I AM TERRIFIED OF MY OWN MIND. The truth is that I'm afraid my memories will kill me. I'm afraid if I never access them, they will kill me, and I'm afraid if I do remember, I can't live with them.

Somehow I stammer that out to Jill Bannerman and she takes some kind of notes and Leona gets her dispensation or whatever it is and I meet the senior staff's advocate, a man named Rory Harper, whom I've seen before, but I can't remember in what context.

He's older, fifties, sixties, silvering hair and a dignity that I don't like. I don't want someone like him to see me go through the tests. I don't want anyone to see me.

But I have no choice.

So I agree to everything, and end up here.

10

YOU NEVER SEE THE WHOLE SHIP, NO MATTER WHAT SHIP you're on. About fifty ships have a specialty. Those ships never go on planetside missions because we don't want to lose them. I got the last of my education on the *Brazza*. The *Brazza* specializes in education, the *Santé* specializes in medical training, the *Eiffel* specializes in engineering, and the *Seul* specializes in officer training, just to name a few.

And even on the *Brazza*, adventurous and young, I never explored the entire ship. No one did, no one could. There was just too much to see, too much to do.

And here, on the *Ivoire*, even though I've worked in the medical wing, I've never seen these rooms.

The testing rooms.

They're dark and strange, buried deep within the ship. They feel like the very center of the ship, even though they cannot be. The *Ivoire*, like all of the ships in the Fleet, have a birdlike design—a narrow, curved front, expanding to massive body in the center with wider sections that seem like wings, and a final tail toward the back. This makes the *Ivoire* sound small, but it is not.

The medical unit is in one of the wider sections, with easy access from several areas of the ship. The unit is several levels down, with a lot of material between it and the exterior, unlike my apartment, which is right on the edge. If an attack destroys a section of the ship, that section mostly will not include the medical unit.

Or these testing facilities.

They seem close, cavelike, and my breath catches as I step inside.

I will be alone in here, with doctors of all kinds, as well as my advocate (Leona) and the ship's advocate (Harper) observing through the walls. Or through something. I am a bit unclear on the mechanism.

Jill assures me that I will be safe, that the monitors in the floor, the walls, the very room itself, will know when I am too emotional to continue, and will pull me back. I will rest, then, and maybe even receive something to help me into a dreamless sleep.

I do not like this room. I do not like the low light, the dark interior, the cushy floor. I want a portal or a screen or something familiar. Before the door closes, I catch her arm.

"Is there somewhere else to do this?"

She shakes her head. "This room is safe."

"I don't like it," I say. "There's nothing here."

She gives me a sad look that I suspect she intended as compassionate. "We need the room to mold around you.

Nothing in here can contradict what's happening inside your mind. That's probably what's making you uncomfortable."

I cannot go inside. I remain in the doorway. "I'm sorry," I say. "I can't do this."

"It will help you."

I shake my head—or rather, I shake my head even more. I don't realize until this moment that I've been shaking my head all along.

"No," I say. "I can't go in this room."

Somehow Leona has found her way to my side. "If she doesn't want to go in, she doesn't have to."

Leona's voice is firmer than mine. Its forcefulness makes my stomach muscles tighten. I feel nauseous.

"People often balk before going in," Jill says. "It's part of the process. Your memories are difficult, and the fear you feel has to do with them, not with the room."

I'm still shaking my head. "No."

Leona slips her arm around my back. She leads me out of the area. Jill follows, uttering soothing words, trying to coerce me back into that room.

I can't. I won't.

We get to the main room—the room that constantly changes—it's white now, with yellow accents—and I burst into tears.

Part of me stands aside and watches myself cry. I don't cry. I can count the number of times I've shed tears, including the day my parents died.

The crying feels alien, as if there is a part of me that I cannot control.

"I'm sorry," I manage.

"It's better," Leona says.

But it's not. I'll be alone, in my room, dealing with the memories all by myself.

At least I'll have a portal.

That views foldspace.

Nothingness.

Becalmed.

11

But the dreams are gone as if they have never been. As if a mere attempt to enter the room has taken the memories from my head and made me feel more human.

I clean up, then I clean the apartment. I find a language in the database, an old language, a dead language (or so they think) and I proceed to learn it, word for ancient word.

I am digging in for forever, when my door chirrups. A preprogrammed signal, the only one I've put in my door's system.

For Coop.

My breath catches. I don't want to see him. I do want to see him. I want him to go away. I want him to tell me everything.

I go to the door, but do not open it. I engage the comm. "You're supposed to be running the ship."

"I am," he says. I recognize that tone. It's constrained—his captain's tone. His I'm-not-alone-so-don't-bother-me-with-personal-stuff tone. "I'm coming in."

He's captain. He can override any command on this ship.

I step back, run a hand over my hair, check my blouse. I've been dressing like a professional ever since I came back, ever since I started my new language, even though I never thought I'd see anyone again. I need the pretense.

I need to think I'll have a use again.

He comes in, and waits as the door closes behind him.

I'm always startled at how much older he looks. Not that command has aged him, although it has, it's just that I remember the boy I fell for, the handsome dark-haired boy full of promise, and now that boy has become a man—a powerful man—who stands before me.

He's wearing his black uniform with silver piping, the everyday uniform, nothing special. He would look normal if it weren't for his hair. He hasn't tended to it in days, and it has grown long, brushing his collar, making him seem almost unkempt.

"They say you're refusing treatment," he says.

I can't tell if this visit is compassionate or a ship problem. I can't tell if he's here because he's my former husband and still my friend, or if he's here because he's the ship's captain, or both.

I'm not sure I should be able to tell.

"I went to them for help, but I can't go in the treatment rooms." It sounds crazy. *I* sound crazy. But I'm beginning to come to terms with that. I think I am crazy.

"The doctors say you're claustrophobic," he says. "That's why you can't go in. You've never been claustrophobic before."

I look at him, a denial about to cross my lips. Then—

—the bodies pile on top of me. I'm drowning in them, afraid to move, afraid not to move, my head wedged in a slightly angled position. I catch some air, but not much. Enough, apparently, to keep me breathing, even though I feel like I'm being crushed.

I curse and realize that I'm sitting down. Coop is crouched before me.

"What was that?" he asks.

I tear up. I blink, hoping that he won't notice. "The memories," I say. Then I take a deep breath, determined to change the subject. "Why are they letting you in here? What if I'm dangerous?"

He smiles. "You're not?"

"The medical evaluation unit thought I was."

"They're wrong," he says.

"You don't know that," I say. "You can't know that."

"You got brainwashed in a month planetside? You've a firm core, remember? No one can brainwash you. That's why you're such a good linguist. You can keep your sense of self while understanding others."

"Anyone can change," I say. My heart is beating hard. "They think I killed twenty-four people."

He has taken my right hand. He holds it gently, and rises just a little so that he's not crouching any more. He sits beside me, like a shy lover, but there's nothing romantic in his posture.

"Twenty-four people died," he says. "And you didn't. That's what we know."

"Why didn't you leave me there?" I ask. "That's protocol."

"I wasn't about to leave you there," he says.

I look at him. I don't know how to respond. So I say, "You should let me look at the communications array."

"I'd love to," he says. "But I can't. Not until we know what you've done."

"What do the others say?"

"They say you abandoned them." His voice is harsh. "They say you left everyone to fend for themselves."

"I would never do that." The words come out of my mouth before I can stop them.

This time his smile is real. "I know," he says. "I think they're lying."

12

Quurzid, the language the Quurzod speak, is a mixture of six different languages we've encountered in this sector. Only the Quurzod have toughened up the words, shortened the syntax, added guttural sounds and some glottal stops that none of the other languages have.

Yet the Quurzod language flows, like music, even with the harshness. Almost because of the harshness—atonal and oddly beautiful, spare, austere, and to the point.

I can hear the Quurzod talking all around me, even though I am not with them. I am sitting in that awful testing room. Coop walked me inside, his arm around my back. His presence reassures me, even though it shouldn't, even though we shouldn't get along. We're not a couple any longer.

Yet some vestiges of couplehood remain.

Coop has left—he's on call, which means if I need him, and he's not handling some emergency, he'll come. But my sister sits outside this room. My twin sister, Deirdre.

We no longer look alike, she and I. We've lived our lives so differently that what once looked identical now just looks familial. If I had lived her life, I would look like her—heavier, settled, smile lines around her mouth. Her hair flows around her face, and her eyes are soft.

Deirdre waits for me in the waiting room, even though she knows this might take a day or more. She doesn't care. She acts as if I'm dying of some dread disease, and for all we know, I am.

Some mental disease.

I have already settled onto the floor of this strange room, but it hasn't curved around me yet. It's waiting for me to give the go-ahead. Because I balked the first time, I get an extra five minutes to reconsider my choice.

I'm not going to change my mind.

The Quurzod whisper around me. If I close my eyes, I'll be able to see them. They met us on a broad plain, the sun setting behind them. It was a dramatic and powerful introduction, the sky blood-red as the light died.

The Xenth warned us that the Quurzod would be dramatic. The Xenth warned us that the Quurzod would lie.

My arms are pressed against my side. Something has punctured the skin in my wrist. My eyes flutter open for a moment, and it becomes clear that the room has absorbed me.

My breath catches in complete panic. My heart races. I want to claw myself out, I want to climb, I need to—

—*get out. Escape. I could die in here. I* will *die in here if I'm not careful. I will disappear and no one will know what happened to me in this bloody silence, this stench, this heat and the pressure and the horrible, horrible*—

"No," I whisper. It takes me a moment to realize I whisper in Quurzid. Unlike most human languages which use simple words, often words of one syllable, for no, Quurzid uses seven syllables for no—a long, complicated word, one that requires a lot of effort to speak correctly. You can't involuntarily finish the word "no" in Quurzid, like you can in Standard. "No" in Standard slips out. In Quurzid, you know what you're saying by the third syllable, and you can leave the word unfinished.

The Quurzid word for "no" is the most deliberate word for "no" in any language I've encountered.

And that's the word I spoke. A deliberate word, one shows I do not now—or ever—want to revisit those memories.

For a moment, I imagine screaming for help, thinking of escape, like they told me to, so that the room will release me. But then I will see my sister's face as I leave, filled with disappointment and fear and concern.

My sister, the caretaker, knows that she will be responsible for me, because she can't *not* be responsible for me, no matter how much I try to keep her out.

I close my eyes as the whispers start again, the Quurzod, talking among themselves as they stood on that ridge. They were half naked, only their arms and legs covered with some kind of paint, a bit of armor across their genitals. The women as well as the men are bare-chested. They show no shame in revealing their bodies, unlike some cultures we've encountered.

Unlike the Xenth.

The Xenth should have been the musical ones. Their language is all sibilants intermingled with soft "ch" sounds and the occasional sighing vowel. But the effect isn't musical. It's creepy, as if something is hissing with disapproval or anger.

Three of our people quit at the prospect of facing the Quurzod, but it was the Xenth who terrified me. The Xenth with their too-thin women, wearing long sleeves and high-neck collars and tight pants that sealed at the ankles, even in the heat. The Xenth, whose men looked at me as if I were not just dressed improperly but suggestively.

I wore a uniform that covered everything except my neck, and I considered coming back to the ship just so that I could get the proper clothing. But our Xenth hosts assured me there was no time. They wanted us to broker some kind of resolution to a fight with them and the Quurzod, a fight over a genocide that had occurred a year before, a fight that could—in the opinion of the Xenth—lead to planetwide war.

We had studied everything, or so we thought. Sixteen different cultures existed on the only continent on Ukhanda. Sixteen different cultures with only two that had the military might to dominate—the Quurzod and the Xenth. The Xenth controlled the plains, but the Quurzod held the mountains. They also controlled most of the airways, giving the Xenth the seas. Both had space flight, but the Quurzod used it to their own advantage.

How the Xenth contacted us, I am not certain. They didn't contact the *Ivoire*. They contacted one of the other ships in our Fleet, and decisions went up the chain of command. The *Ivoire* got involved because of me. Because I am—was—had been—the best linguist in the Fleet.

My heart twists. I open my eyes. The room is the color of that twilight, blood-red and gold, with shadowy figures lining the walls. My stomach turns.

I can't do this. I can't do it. I can't.

But if I don't, I'll die.

I have no idea if the words I'm thinking come from the meeting or that horrible memory of the bodies or come from now. I hate the way my arms press against my sides. I shift, and am surprised that the floor shifts with me. I can—if I want—pull that thing from my wrist, the thing that is going to keep me hydrated and nourished, and flee this place. Go on my own, figure things out by myself. Live my own damn life.

Alone.

Becalmed.

I take a deep breath.

I have never fled from a battle in my life.

I force my eyes closed and let the memories overtake me.

13

I CAME TO THE MEETINGS LATE. LINGUISTS FROM THE flagship, *Alta*, had flanked the diplomats, talking with the Xenth long before I arrived. I got study materials and cultural documents one week before my first meeting, and that meeting was with the Xenth.

The Xenth's capital city, Hileer, was a port city. The buildings on the bay had glass walls facing the water, but deeper inland, the buildings had no windows at all. The Xenth built backwards—or what I thought of as backwards—the tallest buildings by the view with the rest getting progressively shorter the farther away from the water we got. Only doors had glass, and then only a small rectangle, built at eye-level, so that the person inside could see who knocked.

The buildings of state, where the parties and balls and ceremonies were held, stood bayside, but the buildings of government, where the actual governing occurred, were single-story structures miles from the waterline.

The ceilings were low, the doorways lower, and the interiors too dark for my taste. They were also both chilly and stuffy, as if the air got recycled only rarely. Add to that the hissing, scratching sound of the Xenth language, and for the first time in my long and storied career, I felt a distinct on-sight aversion to the people I was meeting.

I had to work to smile, work to touch palms—their version of shaking hands—work to concentrate on their words, instead of their shifting eyes, which were as much a part of their communication as hand gestures were to some cultures. I did learn to understand the eye shifts, but try as I might, I could not add them to my personal repertoire. I apologized in advance, and the Xenth seemed to understand.

I had no real importance to them. I had no real diplomatic importance in that room, anyway. I was there to listen, learn, and discover all I could about the Quurzod.

The Xenth had asked for help with them.

What the Xenth told us that afternoon is this:

Their quarrels with the Quurzod went back five hundred years. Initially, they had border skirmishes that caught almost no attention. Neither the Xenth nor the Quurzod cared much about their shared borders.

They did care about the seas, and sea battles between both countries had become legendary, but rare. Usually the ships passed each other in international waters, threatening, but not following up on the threats.

But travel became easier, as both sides built roads, discovered their own personal air travel, and slowly conquered space. Neither group were nation-builders, at least initially. They didn't want to conquer the other side and take their land. But no one could define exactly what land belonged to whom on those shared borders, and as travel became more commonplace, so did the border skirmishes, which led to many deaths, which led to formal armed hostilities, which led to full-scale warfare at least a dozen times in the past 250 years.

Another culture, the Virrrzd, negotiated the first peace treaty for the Xenth and Quurzod, and it held (tentatively) for thirty years. Then the border skirmishes started up again, along with raids into each other's territories.

The raids went deeper and deeper, growing more and more violent, until the Quurzod committed an out-and-out massacre, killing every single Xenth (man, woman, and child) within one hundred miles of what the Quurzod believed to be the border.

The Xenth immediately called for another peace conference, demanding reparations. The Quurzod came, and as both sides made actual headway, Quurzod along the border died hideously.

The Quurzod claimed they were attacked by an illegal chemical weapon, long banned on Ukhanda. The Xenth claimed that the Quurzod's own building materials had an adverse reaction with chemicals the Xenth used for land cultivation. The Quurzod deaths, the Xenth claimed, were caused by their own greed in gobbling up the land.

The Fleet arrived just as the war along the border was about to escalate again. The *Alta* contacted both sides and offered to broker a deal between them. Only the Xenth took the *Alta* up on it.

The Quurzod were too busy burying their dead.

Or so we were told.

Claims, counterclaims, historical arguments so detailed that even the locals did not understand all of them. The Fleet managed to hold off hostilities by patrolling the border with our own people. We have small fighters that we used to fly over the disputed area, keeping both sides away.

We had maintained that position during the months of negotiation.

Finally, the Quurzod agreed to talks, so long as there would be no activity along the border during that time. *No chance for backstabbing*, or so they said.

My team would go in three months in advance of the diplomats. We would become as Quurzod as possible, learn their culture, their traditions, their rituals. We wouldn't go native—we had learned over the years that too many cultures had found the attempt to go native as deep an insult (or perhaps a deeper insult) than failing to learn the language.

So much of communication is nonverbal. Eye movements like the Xenth had, hand gestures found in so many Earth cultures, smiles or lack thereof in a series of cultures in the previous sector. These things could make or break a delicate negotiation.

I'd heard rumors—impossible to substantiate without talking to the Quurzod themselves—that Quurzid had a four-tiered structure. The first was a formal tier, for strangers within the Quurzod culture. Extremely polite, with its own sentence structure and vocabulary. The second was the familial tier for family and close friends, informal in its sentence structure with a private vocabulary, often known only to the family/friends themselves. The third was street Quurzid, offensive, abrupt, and as violent as the culture. Again, a different sentence structure and vocabulary. Used in threatening situations, among the criminal classes, and by the military in times of war.

Finally, there was diplomatic Quurzid, which bore almost no relation to any of the other forms of Quurzid at all. So far as I could tell, diplomatic Quurzid evolved as a language to speak to enemies, without giving them any insight into the Quurzod at all.

The Virrrzd were the ones who figured that out, which was why they could successfully broker the original deal with the Xenth. But the Virrrzd were unwilling to get involved this time—the conflict between the Xenth and Quurzod had taken such a nasty turn that the Virrrzd were afraid for their own safety.

The Virrrzd knew both formal and diplomatic Quurzid, but not street or familial Quurzid. We felt—the linguists, the diplomats, the Fleet—that the only way to settle this dispute between the Xenth (who had only one language in only one form) and the Quurzod was to quite simply learn to communicate fully with the Quurzod.

Which was why my team got sent in.

14

I SURFACE TO SIBILANTS (*whisper, whisper, hiss, hiss, hiss*) and shudder as I open my eyes. The room is dark and has folded around me. I can't really see anything. My heart pounds. I have no idea how much time has passed.

I'm supposed to get lost in the memories, and maybe I am lost, but it doesn't feel like the kind of lost I expected. It's almost as if I'm having a conversation with someone else, not reliving the past. Not like—

—*clawing, climbing, reaching, bodies rolling beneath my feet, shifting against my hand, the feel of dried blood on my cheek, the cold flesh under my palms. That's lost. I'm lost. I'll never survive—*

I'm holding my breath. I have to make myself breathe, and as I inhale the breath sounds like a sob. The air has a faint tinge of rot—is that what this place does? It mimics what happened?—and I think it'd be so easy to escape, so easy to leave—

Only to live in my room forever. Forever slipping, dreaming, hiding from my own brain, my own memories.

I close my eyes and force myself back inside, force myself to breathe—

***

—THE HOT DRY AIR. A SMALL HEADACHE HAS FORMED between my eyes. The Quurzod are not cordial, although we've been here for weeks. My host family will not talk while I am in the room. I hear them whispering when I am nearby, and I strain to listen. But they use formal Quurzid whenever I'm around.

Fortunately, my team fares better. They have made recordings of Quurzid in all its glory, marking what they believe to be familial Quurzid and what they believe to be street Quurzid.

No Quurzod will tell us the difference. Once the Quurzod figured out that we wanted to know the entirety of their language, they stopped treating us like guests and started treating us as if we were Xenth.

Except for Klaaynch. Klaaynch is thin, reedy, beautiful according to our culture—long blond hair and classic features—but strange to the Quurzod, whose features are thicker, hair generally a dark, almost orangish red. I cannot quite tell how old Klaaynch is. She's one of those girls who looks the same at thirteen as she will at twenty-three.

I'm guessing she's eighteen or so, very curious, with a gift for language. She already speaks some Standard poorly, learned through overheard snatches of discussion.

She reminds me of myself. All ears, wanting to know what everyone is saying, no matter what language they speak.

Her family won't host, so she watches me from afar. I eat in the prescribed visitor restaurants, and stay in the visitor hotel when I am not with my host family. The Quurzod agreed to host families, but balked at overnight stays, and frowned on sharing meals. "Host" is not really a good term for what they're doing, but we have no other. They are sharing as much as they can.

Klaaynch cannot sit with me in a visitor restaurant, and I cannot go to a Quurzod-only place. Sometimes she sits beneath one of the arching trees that mark every intersection. I have learned to eat outside in the visitor restaurants, at the table closest to the tree. Klaaynch and I talk, or try to, and she has promised me she will teach me familial Quurzid.

She says in diplomatic Quurzid (the only Quurzid I know fluently), *They cannot tell me who my friends are. They cannot determine whom I care about and whom I do not. If they try, I shall challenge them.*

I admire her reasoning.

And her courage. She wants to step outside her culture and learn other cultures. She wants to become more than who she is.

Is this what Coop says he saw in me? This desire for knowledge, the desire to add to the core by reaching beyond the training, beyond the culture?

I sit and murmur to Klaaynch, not knowing that her face—

—is the first one I see, rolling toward me, eyes open, mouth gone, as if someone cut it away, those cheekbones crushed, her hair wrapped around her neck. She is buried just above me, thrown on top of me, her blood on my skin—

***

I GASP, AND THIS TIME I AM THINKING OF ESCAPE long before I vocalize it. I claw the floor, the needle poking my skin, the darkness holding me. I climb out and crawl toward the door, nearly there when Jill reaches me. She drags me out of the room as if she's dragging me out of that pit.

I stumble and fall against Deirdre who asks me what's wrong, asks me to talk to her, asks me what I need.

"Leona," I say. "Please. Find Leona."

And then I pass out.

***

AND WAKE IN ONE OF THE HOSPITAL BEDS, LIKE I found myself in after they rescued me on Ukhanda. Leona is there, but not there. She flits in, she flits out. She won't talk to me in the medical wing. She forces me to wait until I am well enough to sit in a conference room without any medical equipment at all. She is even going to bring the chairs.

She knows that I know. She doesn't know *what* I know. Just that I know.

And I ache because of it.

I ache.

15

Cultures do not invent languages and traditions overnight. They evolve over time. And while some linguists believe that the language comes before the culture, I believe that the language serves the culture.

Think of a culture that has developed four different languages, each with a prescribed purpose.

The Xenth, who wear formal clothing and have precise traditions about who may have windows and who may not, who may look to the left and who may not, have but one language, without much more complexity than most human languages.

Twenty-eight letters, millions of words, a simple sentence structure followed in infinite variations.

But the Quurzod, who wear little to no clothing, and have windows everywhere, and few walls in their homes, the Quurzod divide the world with their language.

Language is forbidden to some, and embraced by others.

Language is not just for communicating, but also for protection. Protection of the culture, protection of the family, protection of the Quurzod traditions, whatever they might be.

And whatever they might be, they are precious to the Quurzod.

In my excitement to learn, I forgot about strictures and structures and barriers. I forgot that language conceals as well as reveals. I forgot that protections exist for a reason.

And I forgot what it is like to be young and curious and different from everyone else.

I forgot.

I grew up in a culture that embraces difference, celebrate diversity, and loves outsiders. A culture that believes itself superior to all others, yes, but in an open-minded way, a way that allows curiosity, a way that states the more we learn, the better we are.

I forgot that not everyone sees the universe as broadly as we do.

I forgot that not everyone has seen the universe.

I forgot that not everyone is *allowed* to see the universe.

When we finally get to our private conference room, I tell Leona that she no longer has to defend me. I caused the crisis with the Quurzod. I should have been left behind.

I should have been left to die.

She wants me to explain that, and I do, because I owe her that much. I explain, but haltingly. I do not want to slip into the memories again. But someone has to understand.

Someone has to know.

Besides me.

16

CHILDREN ABSORB LANGUAGE. THEY ARE BORN WITHOUT it, but with the capacity to learn it. Some lose that capacity as they age, or let it atrophy or never really had a great capacity for it at all. But others never lose the ability to absorb language, and consequently, they crave more and more of it.

They want to learn—or maybe they need to learn.

I have always needed to learn. Sounds and syntax are like symphonies to me, and as much as I love the old symphonies, I am always searching for new ones.

Klaaynch needed to learn too. And if all I had done was teach her Standard, we would have been fine. But she wanted to teach me the glories of Quurzid—all of Quurzid—and I wanted to learn.

She might have gotten away with teaching me some familial Quurzid. She was right; no one could choose her friends for her.

But street Quurzid—it was beautiful and complex and revealing, a culture in and of itself, one that revered violence and anger as a way of life. Each word had degrees of meaning depending on how it fell in a sentence, as well as what tone the speaker used (High, low? Soft, loud? Quick, slow?), and each meaning had nuances as well. Street Quurzid was one of those languages that would take weeks to learn and a lifetime to understand.

I was thinking that after I completed my mission as the linguistic diplomat at the peace conference between the Xenth and Quurzod, I would stay on Ukhanda and study street Quurzid. I would spend the rest of my life immersed in the most complex language I had ever heard.

Maybe I mentioned that to someone. Maybe I had merely thought it. Maybe my intentions were clear to people whose language was so complex that my language must have seemed like a child's first halting sentences.

I don't know.

What I do know is this. I convinced Klaaynch to take me to one of the violence pools—a gathering site where the Quurzod train. They live in those places, not in their homes, not in their streets, not in their restaurants or their places of business, but in their violence pools.

Violence pools are little mobile communities. They exist as long as they need to. If they get discovered by outsiders, they move.

Small buildings, assembled out of sticks and cloth, appear, then disappear as needed. They form a circle around a flattened area, and in that flattened area, lessons happen.

Most of the lessons are in things we consider illegal. How to kill someone with a wide variety of weaponry.

How to kill someone with sticks. How to kill someone with fists alone. These are not military lessons, which we also provide, but lessons in survival.

Quurzid, for all its complexity, does not seem to have a word for "murder."

Lessons here are proprietary. Outsiders cannot see them. I did not observe the violence pool during lessons, although I heard about them. The worst, according to Klaaynch, were the defensive lessons. Because if you failed, you would get injured. If you had trouble learning why you failed, you would get injured in the same way repeatedly. If you flinched as someone came at you after you had already been injured once, you were taken off the roster until your psyche healed. If you flinched again after your return, you were relegated to non-violent work—talking, writing, science, mathematics—all of which were seen as inferior.

Klaaynch's dream of being a linguist was considered odd, and it *was* odd, for the Quurzod. The only thing that saved her, the only thing that gave her any kind of power and potential, was her ability to fight.

She was considered the best of her generation.

And she proved it.

It took her four hours to die.

I know because I watched.

It was the only time I had been allowed in an actual violence pool during fighting. I sat behind Klaaynch and her team. *We* sat there, all except the two who escaped. Klaaynch and her young team. Me and mine. Twenty-three lives from the ship, lives I wasted in my attempt to learn the wrong form of Quurzid. Awnings attached to the small buildings shaded us, but the air was hot—hotter than anything I had ever experienced—and dry.

The Quurzod gave us water. They gave us something to keep our fluids balanced. They wanted us to live—at least until the fighting ended.

I was not allowed to speak, and I did not.

Around me, Quurzod I had met—most in their teens, some barely adult—fought for their very survival.

But the match that mattered was Klaaynch's.

It took four hours for their best fighters to kill her. A dozen adults against one thin girl. Four hours.

If she had survived for six hours, she would have lived and been granted favors. One of the favors she wanted was to get permission for me to study street Quurzid.

Not the violence pools themselves.

Just street Quurzid.

And while I did that, she wanted me to teach her Standard. Standard, and all of the other languages I knew.

She was so marvelous. So strong. So brave. So beautiful.

But three hours and forty-five minutes in, someone snapped her right femur. She kept fighting, but she had no base, no way to maintain her balance. At three hours and fifty-eight minutes, she fell.

It took only two minutes to finish her off. The others in her violence pool, those who had been contaminated by me, died that afternoon as well.

The fighters dismantled the buildings. Beneath the largest was the pool itself. A hollow, empty pit in the ground, designed to hold the losers of any large fight.

Klaaynch had told me this as we waited for the others to show up. She told me that the pools often were not used, and when the time came to move the violence pool, the actual pool itself got filled.

This one got filled too.

With us.

Most of my team fought back. When it became clear that we would die, they fought. But they were no match for the Quurzod.

They went into the pool. Then me, then Klaaynch's friends.

And finally, Klaaynch.

No one touched me, except to knock me unconscious. It should have been enough to kill me. In the heat, among the dead, in the dryness.

I should have died.

But I did not.

17

To her credit, Leona does not speak as I tell my story. She tries to keep her face expressionless, but she cannot control her eyes. They narrow, they widen. Several times, she keeps them closed for a few extra seconds, as if she does not want to look at me any more.

I don't want to look at me either.

"The other two, they were right," I say. "I caused this. I'm why we're here. Becalmed."

Leona does not nod. Nor does she reach out a hand to comfort me. She sighs. "They abandoned their post."

They did. They left the Quurzod as the rest of us went to the violence pool. They should have stayed with us, but they thought something might go wrong and they fled.

I should have told the others to go as well. The mistake was mine, not theirs.

"It doesn't matter," I say. "I shouldn't be here."

"The Captain decides that," she says. "He brought you back."

"When he didn't have all of the information," I say.

She inclines her head. She is conceding that point.

"Tell him I'm ready. He can't send me back, but he shouldn't keep me here either."

"You're volunteering for execution?" she asks.

"It's the right thing," I say.

"I don't think that's your decision," she says. "Not anymore."

18

THEY RETURN ME TO MY QUARTERS. THE APARTMENT NO longer looks like mine. I recognize everything in it, I even remember hanging the quilt, scrunching the blanket on my divan, but the place feels strange to me, like a memory that I have abandoned. The apartment has a dusty odor, as if I've been gone for months, which is impossible. First of all, I have not been gone more than a few days, and secondly, the air gets recycled in here. Nothing should smell of dust.

I make myself dinner and sit in one of the chairs to eat it. Normally, I would play a language quiz or watch an entertainment, but I do neither. I sit and listen.

The Quurzod whisper all around me. The sound infects me, like the memories infected me. The memories are there, but I no longer slip into them accidentally. Instead, I roll them around in my mind, worrying them, like my tongue would worry a chipped tooth.

No wonder I blocked them. All those people, dead because of me. Because I did not understand—when I am trained to understand.

I should have known. I should have figured it out.

And I did not.

Not even when Klaaynch said to me that she could chose her own friends. When she said it with defiance, with that glow the rebellious get as they anticipate a fight.

If the Quurzod so strongly protect the language they use for family and friends, it should have seemed obvious to me that they would viciously defend the language they strove to keep secret. I should have known—maybe I did know—of course I knew.

And that is why I blocked the memories.

I didn't want to remember that feeling—that I'll-deal-with-it-later feeling—the one I ignored.

I have been sitting with my plate in my lap for nearly an hour when the door chime sounds. Coop's chime.

It does not surprise me. A part of me has expected to see him all along.

He looks big, powerful, as he comes through that door. His presence is almost too much for the room.

"Leona tells me you volunteered for execution." He does not sit. He towers over me. "I won't do it."

"It's regulation." I clutch the plate. I have not really moved, except that my muscles have tensed.

"Regulation is what the captain says it is," he says.

I shake my head slightly. "If that were true, each ship would be a tiny dictatorship."

He sits on the divan across from me, balancing on the edge, leaning toward me. "It's not like you to give up."

I look at him. When we met, I predicted the lines that formed around his eyes. But the one that furrows his brow is a surprise; he frowns more than I would have ever expected.

"I haven't given up," I say. Even when I should have. I'm the one who caused this, not him. I'm the one who didn't die in that pit. I'm the one who climbed out—over bodies, over people I knew. I'm the one who staggered through that desert, to the borders where I knew the Xenth would find me. I'm the one who made it to that village, against all odds.

I did not give up.

And I should have.

"You haven't thought it through," he says. "They tricked us."

I blink, frown, then get up. I walk the plate to the recycling unit. If I don't eat that food, someone else should get the nutrients.

"They didn't trick me," I say with my back to him. "I went to that violence pool of my own free will."

"Not the Quurzod," he says. "The Xenth."

I turn. I didn't deal with the Xenth. Most of the negotiations with the Xenth happened before I was brought into the discussions.

I am suddenly cold.

He's looking at his hands. "They tricked all of us."

I walk back and sit down. I wait.

He raises his head. Those lines, those sad eyes.

"Think about it," he says. "The imbalance of power that has existed there for centuries. Then, one day, a fleet of ships arrives, a fleet with more power than the Xenth can imagine. And we offer to help."

He twists his hands together. He has thought of this for a long time.

"They ask the initial negotiators, they say—"

"*If we ask you to obliterate the Quurzod, you would do so?*" I whisper this in Xenth. I have read the documentation. They did say that, and the initial negotiators wrote it off as a test.

I believed the initial negotiators. After all, they're the ones on the ground. They watch body language. They know the culture—or should know the culture. They're the ones who understand what is going on.

Besides, the Xenth's question wasn't unusual. Every culture we encounter wants to know our limits. Our limits are that we help, we do not engage.

Unless we are engaged first.

Coop quotes the line, ignoring my Xenth, which he does not understand. He is used to me muttering in other languages. I have done it as long as he has known me. "We refuse to destroy Quurzod. We spend time studying the situation, and then we offer our diplomatic services to the Xenth. But during the time we studied them, the Xenth studied us."

So buttoned up, so formal and proper. Hidden, too, but we should have expected that.

Only that isn't my mistake. I wasn't with the initial group. The initial groups came from elsewhere in the Fleet, and somehow they overcame—or maybe never had—their aversion to the Xenth, and their hissing, sibilant-filled language.

I, on the other hand, never trusted them.

But I did trust my commanders. I trusted my orders, figuring they all knew the history, the facts, the personalities of both sides.

"The Xenth knew," Coop says. "They knew about the violence; they've suffered from it. They accused the Quurzod of massacres, not telling us that this was part of Quurzod culture, that they kill anyone—regardless of nationality—if they violate certain rules. The Xenth made sure we did not know those rules. They sent us in blind."

It is so easy to blame another culture. But I shake my head. I believe in mistakes before I believe in deviousness.

"That can't be true," I say. "The Xenth left too much to chance."

"They left nothing to chance," he says. "If we had actually figured out a way to negotiate with the Quurzod, the Xenth would have gained a solid border, some defined territory, an end to a long war. But if we did not find a way to negotiate, if we aggravated the Quurzod, the Quurzod would come after us. They would have *engaged* us—"

"And the Xenth's war would have become our war," I say. He's right. The logic is inescapable. It explains my unease. It explains the lack of preparation the Fleet's diplomatic team gave to my team. The Fleet's team was tricked.

I don't usually believe in the duplicity of other cultures, but this is too big a mistake to miss—at least on the part of the Xenth. And I understand the Fleet's diplomacy well enough to know that had we understood the extreme violence of the Quurzod, no one would have sent my team in unprotected.

"The Xenth's war did become our war," Coop says. "Only the rest of the Fleet fights it while we wait here."

"We don't know if they're fighting it," I say.

He stares at me. We know. They're fighting it. And while the Quurzod are fierce on the ground, they are no match for the Fleet in space.

The Quurzod will fight brilliantly, like Klaaynch did. And then the Fleet will destroy something important, destroy the Quurzod's balance.

And they will die within minutes, leaving the Xenth to fill the void.

Without us, the Fleet will think they have done the right thing.

I look at Coop. He smiles, just a little, hesitant, more the boy I remember than the man he is.

"If you knew all of this," I say, "why didn't you tell me? Why did you let me stay locked in here, with the doubts and the memories?"

"I suspected," he says. "I had no proof. I just knew you, and your core, and how you would never, ever betray any of us, nor would you knowingly jeopardize children."

"They weren't really children," I say softly.

"They weren't yet adults either," he said.

I nod. I will always carry them—the twenty-three members of my team, and the dozen young friends of Klaaynch, and Klaaynch herself. They died for my curiosity, for my ever-solid core.

"It would've been easier if you executed me," I say softly.

He puts his hands over mine. His hands are warm. He says, "Anyone who commands lives with these moments."

I shudder. "But I'm done. I've made my mistake. I should have known—"

"No," he says. "The mistake wasn't yours. In fact, you have done the one thing that might help us."

"What's that?" I ask.

"You learned street Quurzid."

I shake my head. "I don't know street Quurzid. I know as much street Quurzid as the first contact team knows when it goes into a new situation. A phrase here and there, nothing more."

"That's not what your memory says. Your memory knows street Quurzid. You might not be able to speak it, but you have enough of it to help us."

I want to pull my hands from his. I never want to go near street Quurzid again.

"How?" I ask.

"When we get back, you can tell the Quurzod in all of their languages how we both got betrayed."

"And have them destroy the Xenth?" I am appalled.

"Yes," he says so softly that I can barely hear him. This is not the idealistic man I met on *Brazza*. This man is ruthless, utterly ruthless.

"But the Quurzod, they're horrible people," I say.

He studies me.

I wait, but tap my finger ever so slightly. I have lost the gift of patience somewhere. It vanished in that desert.

"You're confusing their culture with ours," he says.

I flush. I used to say that to him. So young. So idealistic. I would say, *One culture cannot judge another until they have a deep understanding of all parts of the culture.*

Including the language, he would say, his eyes sparkling.

And the history, and the things that have developed that culture. Just because they have evolved a tradition that we disagree with doesn't make our position right.

"It's not the same," I say.

"It is," he says.

"The Quurzod *murder* each other," I say.

"So do we," he says. "You asked me to murder you."

"I asked you to execute me, according to our laws."

He waits. Dammit, he has the patience now.

He waits.

He has made his point.

My shoulders slump. We know each other well enough that he understands my capitulation without my verbal acknowledgement.

"I need you to master street Quurzid," he says.

"I don't know enough of it," I say.

"Then do your best," he says. "You need to become *the* expert in Quurzid. Then you need to figure out how to teach our people the language."

"Not just those on the *Ivoire*," I say.

"I want a plan of instruction, something recorded, so that all of the ships in the Fleet can learn it," he says. "I want us to be ready as soon as someone hears our distress call. I want to be able to end the fighting around Ukhanda immediately."

His hands are still around mine. He shakes, just a little, as he says that.

"You think we'll get out of this, then?" I ask.

"Are you asking if we'll be becalmed forever?"

I nod.

"No," he says.

"But you put us on rations," I say.

"It might be a week," he says. "It might be a year. I want to be prepared."

"The Quurzod damaged the *anacapa* drive, didn't they?"

"While we were engaging it," he says. "It'll take some time to figure out what exactly went wrong. That's why I need you."

"Me?"

He nods, and his hands tighten around mine. "I need you to figure out what's wrong with the communications array. I'm convinced our distress signals aren't getting through.

I flush, then let out a small breath. "You trust me to get back to work?"

His gaze meets mine. "Mae," he says, "I've trusted you all along."

He has. He's been the only one. I didn't even trust myself.

I bow my head, stunned at his faith in me. Stunned that I still have a future.

He stands, puts his hands on my shoulder, and kisses the top of my head.

"Welcome back," he whispers.

I lean into him for just a moment.

"It's good to be back," I say, with more relief than I expected, and resist the urge to add, *You have no idea how good it is.*

Because I have a hunch he does know, and that's why he didn't leave me behind.

Because I am still part of the ship. A necessary part of the ship.

And you never abandon the necessities. No matter how difficult it is to retrieve them.

Read more in Kristine Kathryn Rusch's award-winning
Diving Universe, starting with the first novel in the
series, *Diving into the Wreck*, on sale now.

Be the first to know!

Just sign up for the Kristine Kathryn Rusch newsletter,
and keep up with the latest news, releases
and so much more—even the occasional giveaway.

So, what are you waiting for?
To sign up go to kristinekathrynrusch.com.

But wait! There's more. Sign up for the WMG
Publishing newsletter, too, and get the latest news
and releases from all of the WMG authors and lines,
including Kristine Grayson, Kris Nelscott, Dean
Wesley Smith, *Fiction River: An Original Anthology
Magazine, Pulphouse Fiction Magazine, Smith's
Monthly,* and so much more.

To sign up, go to wmgpublishing.com.

ABOUT THE AUTHOR

New York Times bestselling author Kristine Kathryn Rusch writes in almost every genre. Generally, she uses her real name (Rusch) for most of her writing. Under that name, she publishes bestselling science fiction and fantasy, award-winning mysteries, acclaimed mainstream fiction, controversial nonfiction, and the occasional romance. Her novels have made bestseller lists around the world and her short fiction has appeared in eighteen best of the year collections. She has won more than twenty-five awards for her fiction, including the Hugo, *Le Prix Imaginales*, the *Asimov's* Readers Choice award, and the *Ellery Queen Mystery Magazine* Readers Choice Award.

To keep up with everything she does, go to kriswrites.com and sign up for her newsletter. To track her many pen names and series, see their individual websites (krisnelscott.com, kristinegrayson.com, retrievalartist.com, divingintothewreck.com, fictionriver.com, pulphousemagazine.com).

The Retrieval Artist Universe
(Reading Order)